Hotwife Erotic Short Story

First Time Cuckold - Wifey Plays with Hubby's Hot Best Friend

Amber Carden

It was a pleasant Saturday morning. Ethan woke up a little earlier than usual today. It often happened to him that he woke up early on weekends. Ethan took a nap while sitting on the bed. He saw his wife Lily lying on the bed near him. She was still sleeping. Lily's hair was scattered over her face. Ethan was smiling at his wife who was still in deep sleep.

Ethan looked at the wall clock. It was nine o'clock in the morning. He got up and went to the washroom to take a shower.

The weather was pleasant. It was the beginning of winter. He was humming while taking a shower. Ethan and Lily had been married for a long time. Both of them loved each other immensely, but the intensity of their sexual relations was decreasing. Ethan was also a bit worried.

He had absolutely no idea how to improve his married life.

In the next ten minutes, he took a shower and put on trousers and a shirt. As he entered the bedroom, he glanced at Lily. She was still sleeping.

"So deep sleep," Ethan muttered.

He walked over to the dressing table and combed his hair.

During this time, he could not see the perfume. Ethan realized that Lily often misplaced his things. He was looking for perfume in cupboards and drawers. Suddenly he opened a cupboard and saw a beautiful book. This book Ethan had never seen before. He picked up the book and looked at it with interest. After looking at the list, he realized that it was Lily's diary.

He opened a few pages. After reading a few lines, Ethan realized that Lily had written about her life in the book.

"It would be interesting to get to know my wife more deeply," he thought.

Now Ethan didn't have to look for perfume. Now this book had become the focus of his interest. He took the book and sat on the couch.

Ethan flipped through the pages. In one place he saw his friend Mark's name written. Ethan is shocked to read that Lily has confessed her feelings for Mark. Ethan had a curious look on his face. He looked at Lily still sleeping. Reading this paragraph.

"Of course, Ethan's friend Mark has a very attractive personality. He's been the center of my attention since I met him for the first time after marriage. It would be a dream for me if I could get close to him. Those are beautiful moments whenever he comes with Ethan. I'm obsessed with his body. I can't stay away from him. His smile is my weakness. I love you, Mark!"

Ethan read this paragraph with interest. Suddenly Lily changed her crotch. Ethan looked at her but she fell asleep again.

Ethan had a surprised expression on his face. He didn't expect that at all. He never dreamed that his wife Lily had feelings for his friend Mark. He looked at the next paragraph. His curiosity was piqued.

"Last weekend night when Mark came over with Ethan, I was super excited. He was wearing black jeans and a shirt. He was sitting on the sofa when I walked into the room with a drink. I was wearing a tight shirt. So he could see my sexy body. He looked at me for a few seconds and then he turned to Ethan. I wish there was a time when Ethan wasn't home and I had to spend a memorable night with Mark in my bedroom. I believe it is my imagination and this may never be possible in reality. I love his gray beard and pale blue eyes."

Ethan's heart began to beat faster as he read this paragraph. He was shocked to read his wife's emotions and thoughts, but surprisingly, there was no anger on her face. Ethan thought for a while. His curiosity grew as to how he would experience the scene if it actually happened. For a few seconds, he thought. Ethan decided to do the same thing in front of him. However, he wanted to discuss the matter further with Lily. There was interest and curiosity rather than an element of anger in him.

Suddenly Lily sat on the bed. Ethan hid the diary under a pillow on the sofa.

"Good morning honey," he addressed Lily.

"Oh you're awake as always," Lily said, ruffling her hair.

"You take a shower honey and let's have breakfast," Ethan replied cheerfully.

"Okay, honey I'll make breakfast then," Lily replied and went to the washroom.

Once again, Ethan began reading Lily's notes for Mark. It was all very interesting to him. He thought that if Lily agreed, he would also join the game and sit by and watch Lily enjoy herself, but this was only possible after discussing it with Lily.

In about fifteen minutes Lily came back. Her hair was wet. She was wearing trousers and a shirt. Her round boobs were clearly visible in the wet shirt.

"I'll make the tea," Lily looked at Ethan.

"Sure," Ethan smiled.

Lily went into the kitchen. Ethan was looking at her. Her round white face, long black hair, and tall height made her attractive, but shortly after Ethan and Lily's marriage, the sexual relationship between Ethan and Lily was not as intense as before, but he still loved Lily immensely.

Within a few minutes, Lily came out of the kitchen. In her hand was a tray with two cups of tea and some slices.

"Let's have breakfast dear," Lily said pleasantly.

"Of course, only on the weekends do we get to have a leisurely breakfast together," Ethan smiled.

They were having breakfast together. Ethan was living a happy life with his wife, but during this time he was somewhat lacking in intensity and passionate sex. Both of them were worried about it. They would just fall asleep after a few minutes of formal sex, which was a bit disappointing for both of them. But today, Ethan was a bit excited to know Lily's emotions and feelings about Mark.

In no time they both had breakfast. Suddenly, Ethan took Lily's diary off the pillow and placed it on the table.

"What is this honey?" He looked at her.

"Oh this is my personal diary," Lily nervously picked up the diary.

"Dear, can't I read this?" Ethan looked at her.

Lily had a mixed expression of surprise and worry on her face.

"Have you read it?" Lily asked. She looked a little confused.

"Yeah I've read all about your Mark," Ethan revealed.

"Oh my god," Lily covered her face with her diary. Her face turned pale due to embarrassment.

"Lily, you don't have to worry. I'm just curious," Ethan said in a serious tone.

Lily put down the diary. Now her face was covered with diary but her eyes were visible.

"Why are you curious?" Lily asked.

Ethan looked into her eyes. He could see the expression of uncertainty in her eyes. Lily had no idea that Ethan would read everything about Mark in her diary.

"I wonder if you're really interested in Mark?" Ethan asked.

Lily was silent for a while. She didn't know how to respond.

"Lily I have something to ask you. I'm not against your feelings at all," Ethan kept his tone as gentle as possible.

"Ethan. It's my fantasy. Nothing more," Lily replied nervously.

"I've read everything. I can see how interested you are in Mark," Ethan said softly.

Lily placed her diary on her lap. She had no answer.

"If you're really interested in Mark, I don't have a problem," Ethan encouraged her.

"Ethan, I don't think so at all. I've already told you that it's just my fantasy," Lily denied.

"Lily, I don't mind if you actually think all of this," Ethan held her hand. He had a smile on his face.

"Ethan, yes I think so," she admitted.

Ethan stared at Lily for a few seconds. After Lily's confession, he was a little more surprised, but there was no angry expression on his face.

"Okay, Lily. I don't mind at all. If Mark agrees, your dream will come true," Ethan replied with a smile.

"Really, I think it is impossible" Lily looked at Ethan in surprise. He couldn't believe that Ethan would agree.

"Lily, you know I love you so much," Ethan squeezed her hand gently.

"I'm ready to do anything you want," Ethan continued.

"It's really unbelievable to me," Lily smiled.

"Lily, I guess our physical relationship isn't as good as it used to be," Ethan admitted.

Lily was looking at him with her beautiful eyes. They were both sitting facing each other on the couch.

"I think it would be interesting and exciting for us if it all worked out," Ethan offered her.

"What do you think?" Lily questioned.

"I want Mark and you to have romance together in front of me," Ethan replied.

"Oh I really don't believe it," Lily was extremely surprised.

"Lily, it would be interesting for me if I had a friend make out with you in front of me and quench your thirst for sex," Ethan explained.

"Ethan I still love you a lot. But I'm really interested in Mark. Having sex with him would be a really interesting experience for me," Lily expressed her feelings for the first time.

"My dear wife, I think it would improve our sexual relations too," Ethan leaned forward and kissed Lily.

"Oh, if something happens like this, of course, it will work for us too," Lily had a smile on her face.

"Lily, I want to see this scene up close too. I want to enjoy the scene when Mark will fuck you," Ethan said excitedly.

"That would be quite interesting," Lily replied cheerfully.

"I'll discuss this with Mark. I'll invite him to dinner tonight if he agrees," Ethan informed her with his plan.

"Really tonight?" Lily asked excitedly.

"Oh yes, today is Saturday. The next day is Sunday. Tonight will be memorable for us," Ethan replied.

"Would Mark agree to spend the night with me?" Lily questioned. Ethan could feel the excitement in her eyes.

"I can't say for sure. Mark is my friend and would be especially willing to fuck a sexy woman like you," Ethan winked.

Lily smiled back.

"Okay Ethan, I'll be anxiously awaiting Mark's response," she replied.

"Lily, we'll discuss this with Mark after dinner. You make a great dinner today and make yourself attractive to Mark," Ethan explained.

"Okay honey," she leaned forward and kissed him.

Today was Saturday. Ethan had to go to the market to get some household goods but returned in the evening. On reaching home he found that Lily was extremely happy. Mark decorated the bedroom on the second floor. It was an exhibition room that was rarely used but had valuable beds and furniture. After decorating this room, he went to rest in the bedroom on the first floor. Meanwhile, at Lily's request, he invited Mark to dinner, which he accepted.

Lily almost had dinner ready. He showered and put on tight jeans and a shirt. She wanted to make herself attractive to Mark. She went to the second floor with her wet hair. She had to prepare a few more dishes, but she had already prepared dinner.

It was evening time. Lily reached the second floor. She was standing on the balcony looking at the bustling streets of the city. Due to the weekend, people were out in large numbers to enjoy themselves, but most of them were couples. They were walking around holding each other's hands. Suddenly a gust of wind hit her face.

"Life is so beautiful," she smiled.

Lily went to the bedroom on the second floor. This room looked really great. Mark and Lily often spent weekends in the same bedroom after marriage. Lily was surprised to see that Ethan had placed candles on the cupboards. Apart from this, fresh rose flowers were scattered on the bed. There was also a comfortable chair in this room. She understood that Ethan was also excited about tonight.

After inspecting the room, Lily came out. She saw the sun which was about to set. After sunset today, one of his dreams was about to come true.

Lily had a smile on her face. Now it was getting dark. She was going to the first floor slowly. She wore double sole shoes while her long hair was left loose. She reached the first floor. Ethan was in the bedroom. There was an LCD on the wall in front on which an adventure movie was playing.

"Honey, are you ready for dinner?" Ethan asked.

"Oh yes, everything will be finalized in a little while," Lily replied with a smile.

"Mark often compliments your dishes. I hope you make a great one today," Ethan said in a meaningful tone.

"Sure," Lily replied and walked into the kitchen.

She had finalized everything in half an hour. Meanwhile, she was thinking about tonight. Although she was excited, she was quite confused. She didn't understand how she would perform in front of her husband, but she wanted to feel Mark very close.

In no time Lily went back to the dressing table. She fixed her hair and applied a light lipstick on her lips. Ethan watched with interest as his wife prepared for Mark.

"Ethan I'm a little confused," Lily said.

She sat down on the bed next to Ethan. Her ass was touching Ethan's legs.

"I guess you don't need to be confused. I'll help you," Ethan replied with a frown.

"I'm confused about how Mark and I will perform in front of you," Lily said.

"Oh but I'm excited to see you both together," Ethan replied.

He sat down on the bed next to Lily.

"Really?" Lily asked.

"Yeah, I will be lucky if I get a chance to watch my lovely wife being fucked by my Friend," Ethan said, placing his hands on Lucky's shoulders.

"Oh, I'm really confused Ethan," Lily said again.

"You can't understand my feelings. You should be happy that your husband will watch and help you," Ethan said, kissing her on the shoulder.

Lily closed her eyes. For the first time after marriage, she seemed so passionate about something and it was an interesting experience for her. As time passed by, their excitement was increasing.

After a half hour, the doorbell rang.

"I think Mark has arrived. You should open the door," Ethan told her.

"Ok I see," Lily went to the door.

She opened the door. The next moment her heart was beating fast. Mark was standing in front of her.

"Hello Lily," Mark greeted warmly.

"Hi Mark," she smiled. Feeling Mark's hand in hers sent a wave of excitement through her body.

"Come in," Lily made way for him.

"Thanks," Mark smiled and entered. They both walked into the bedroom.

"Long time no see, my man," Ethan hugged Mark.

"I miss you too Ethan," Mark smiled.

Lily was watching them both. They both sat on the couch. Lily also sat down next to Ethan.

"Why did you arrange dinner for me?" Mark asked.

"Oh, you're so interesting, Mark. It's really amazing to spend the weekend with you," Ethan said with a laugh.

"I also like to have dinner at home rather than at a restaurant," said Mark.

"Dear I think we get to spend a lot of time with each other too," Ethan replied.

"I hope Lily is enjoying her life too," Mark looked at Lily.

"Oh yes," She replied immediately. However, her heart rate was fast.

"Great, I'm glad you both are so happy in your marriage life," Mark looked at Ethan.

"You enjoy together, I'll bring dinner," Lily stood up.

"Sure," Ethan replied.

Meanwhile, Lily got up and went to the kitchen. Through the kitchen window, she was watching Mark and Ethan. Meanwhile, she was hearing their laughter. Mark was wearing a pant coat. Lily looked carefully at him, no doubt he was very handsome. Lily's heart beat faster at the thought that she was going to spend tonight with Mark. Lily was wearing black jeans and a shirt while Mark was wearing a black pent coat and Ethan was in a trouser-shirt.

Lily put all the dishes in the tray and went into the living room. She placed the tray on the table.

"Let's have dinner," she smiled.

Mark looked at her. Once again their eyes met. Mark was a little confused that Lily looked a bit prettier and sexier today.

"Looks great," he commented looking at the dishes.

"If you have a beautiful wife and she can cook great dishes, there's no greater blessing," Ethan said with a laugh.

"Really, you're lucky Ethan," Mark replied.

Lily smiled. They were both admiring her.

"Let's have dinner," Ethan said.

Lily had put everything on the table. They all started having dinner. Even during this time, they were talking. Lily was looking at Mark with lustful eyes. However, sometimes Mark also looked at her, but he looked a bit confused. Soon they had dinner.

"Dinner was really delicious. Thanks, Lily," Mark smiled at her.

"I'm glad you like my dishes," Lily replied.

Ethan was smiling as he was enjoying their conversations.

"I think it's time for a drink," Ethan said.

"Sure, why not," Mark replied.

"Okay, I'll bring the whiskey," Lily said.

She knew Mark was watching her. She walked into the kitchen moving her ass in a sexy way. She took a bottle of whiskey from the fridge poured three glasses and went into the bedroom. Her long hair, pink lips, and brown eyes made her a sexy lady.

They all clinked their glasses and took a sip. They were talking while drinking whiskey.

"Mark I had to discuss something with you," Ethan said suddenly.

"Something special," Mark asked taking a sip of his whiskey.

"You know me and Lily Sack love each other so much," Ethan prefaced.

Mark was watching him with interest. Lily was sitting cross-legged next to Ethan.

"Lily and you are going to spend the night in my bedroom," Ethan revealed.

"Oh god, how is that possible?" Mark asked in surprise. He didn't expect this from Ethan at all. Lily was also looking at him carefully.

"Lily is interested in you Mark, I feel like there's no sexual intensity between us. You have to please my wife," Ethan explained.

"Lily...," Mark looked at her.

"Yes Mark I'm ready," Lily shrugged.

"I'm going to enjoy this whole scene. I want to see Lily excited during romance and sex," Ethan replied.

"I wonder Ethan, would you watch your wife have sex with me?" Mark looked at him with curiosity.

"Oh, yes it was decided by us in mutual consultation," Ethan replied.

"Exactly," Lily agreed.

"Are you ready for this?" Ethan asked Mark.

Mark still had a surprised expression on his face. He was completely unaware of Ethan and Lily's plan. He was deep in thought.

"I guess you shouldn't think too much Mark," Lily held Mark's hand.

Ethan saw his wife holding Mark's hand. It was an interesting scene for him.

"Okay, I'm ready for your pleasure," Mark replied, placing the empty glass on the table.

"Thank you so much Mark, I was sure you wouldn't let me down," Ethan warmly shook Mark's hand.

"Oh Ethan, I'm always with you," Mark replied.

"Tonight we're going to spend this special night in the bedroom on the second floor," Ethan informed her.

Meanwhile, Lily began to take the dishes off the table, but she was looking at Mark with lustful eyes.

"Let's go," Ethan stood up.

Ethan gave Lily's hand to Mark's.

"You have to go together," Ethan said.

Mark and Lily looked at each other with surprise and held hands. They were climbing the stairs. Ethan was behind them. He looked very emotional seeing her wife holding Mark's hand.

As soon as they reached the room on the second floor, they were greeted by an overwhelming aroma.

"Wow, great," Mark said, looking around the room.

Ethan lit the candles in the bedroom. The room was semi-dark. Lily was blushing a little. Mark sat on the bed holding her hand.

Ethan picked up a box of flowers and threw it at Lily and Mark. These were rose flowers. The fragrance was wafting throughout the room.

"Oh my god, thank you, Ethan," Lily said, putting her hand over her mouth. She was looking surprised.

Now Ethan picked up a chair and sat in the corner.

"Come on Mark, Lily is my wife. We'll get closer after seeing all this. I want to deepen my relationship with her in this way," Ethan expressed his feelings.

Lily was smiling. Mark held her hand. Both of them were now standing on the floor. Suddenly Mark put his hands on her shoulders and placed his lips on Lily's forehead. Lily was excited to feel Mark's lips on her forehead. She put her hands on Mark's waist and pulled him closer to her. Mark hugged her. They both started sucking each other's lips.

Ethan was surprised to see this scene. His wife was kissing his friend. Ethan had his full attention. The night had deepened. Only the sound of lip-sucking echoed in the room. Mark's cock was starting to harden. He began to squeeze her ass. Lily's soft ass was making him even more excited.

"You're so sexy," Mark whispered.

Meanwhile, Lily's breathing became faster. She was completely focused on sucking Mark's lips. She was sucking Mark's lips intensely. Ethan leaned forward to see Lily sucking Mark's tongue. Meanwhile, Lily took off Mark's coat and threw it at Ethan. Ethan grabbed the coat and placed it on a nearby table. And again began to look with interest. Lily was breathing fast. Now Mark was kissing her neck. Lily's long hair was in his face.

"Lily, how are you feeling?" Ethan asked.

"Your friend is so hot," Lily commented.

Mark kissed Lily's cheek and sniffed her shirt. Meanwhile, his hand was on Lily's ass. Lily's pussy was starting to get wet.

Ethan was watching them with interest. Lily's excited moans were making him excited. After a long time, he was looking at his wife so passionately.

"Your wife is very sexy Ethan," Mark squeezed her ass.

"Ah, kiss me," Lily breathed deeply.

Ethan smiled. Mark's hands were moving over her tight jeans. Lily moved forward and started kissing Mark on the neck. Her hair was scattered over Mark's face.

"Mark, fuck me, put my pussy on fire," Lily whispered. Her lips were on Mark's white neck. There were signs of Lily's lips on Mark's neck. Lily ran her hand over Mark's chest, unbuttoning his shirt. Ethan was watching Lily's trembling hands. Mark held her head and placed his lips on Lily's again. Once again they both started sucking each other's lips. Meanwhile, Lily had unbuttoned Mark's shirt.

She was now exploring Mark's chest with her soft hands. Ethan realized that they both had their eyes closed. Ethan was very surprised that Lily was so excited. He was feeling relaxed during this. His wife was crazy about having sex with his friend.

Meanwhile, Lily took off Mark's shirt and threw it at Ethan. Ethan put the shirt on the table. He noticed that Mark and Lily were about the same height, but Lily was wearing double shoes.

"I love your muscular body," Lily whispered.

She was now licking Mark's chest. Her long hair was disheveled. Mark was running his fingers through her hair. Ethan felt for a moment as if he was dreaming but it was a reality that his wife was kissing Mark's chest.

Suddenly Mark sprang into action. He held Lily by the waist and laid her on the bed. He now turned to her shows. He tried to take off Lily's shoes.

"Relax my friend, I'm here to help you," Ethan leaned forward.

He took off his wife's shoes with the utmost delicacy and sat back in his chair.

"Wow your wife's feet look so beautiful," Mark said as he placed his lips on her feet.

"Ah," Lily closed her eyes.

Mark was licking her feet. Her feet were white and soft. Ethan was watching the scene with curiosity. He had never romanced Lily so passionately.

"Ah, lick," Lily said as she held Mark's hair. Ethan's eyes were on Lily's face. She was breathing deeply.

Mark pulled Lily's jeans up and started licking her legs.

"I'm going to lick your whole body," Mark said excitedly.

"My wife is yours tonight. Do whatever you want," Ethan gave him freedom.

"Ah, yes Mark, I'm yours. I'm glad my husband is enjoying the scene," Lily murmured.

"Mark, fuck me please, I'm going crazy," Lily whispered.

Mark undid the belt of her jeans and tossed it to Ethan. Ethan caught it and placed it on the table.

Then Mark put his hand inside to massage her pussy.

"Oh your pussy is so wet," Mark commented. His fingers were moving over Lily's pussy.

"Yes, I'm getting hot Mark," Lily leaned forward and kissed Ethan on the lips.

Mark's cock tightened as he felt Lily's warm lips on his.

Ethan had a meaningful smile on his face.

"I can't wait any longer, dear Mark," Lily said and pushed him on the bed. Mark lay down on the bed.

"Oh, you are so smart," Mark said with a laugh.

"You have to fuck me hard tonight," Lily replied and rode on him. Her ass was on the Mark.

Ethan smiled as he saw his wife sitting on his friend. He was extremely happy that his wife was performing so enthusiastically.

Mark was feeling Lily's soft ass at his body. Although they both were wearing jeans, Mark kept his hands on her ass. Lily was all excited. Mark was slowly seducing her but she soon wanted to play with his cock.

"I wanna feel your cock in my hand," she looked at Mark.

"Tonight, I am with you. We will do everything," Mark replied.

Lily took his head in her hands and placed her warm lips on Mark's lips in response.

"Oh, I love to take the control," she whispered and started sucking Mark's lips. Mark was pressing her ass lovingly. Lily began to moan softly.

Seeing this scene, Ethan's cock began to harden, but he wanted to enjoy watching his wife having sex with Mark today.

"I think your husband is lucky to have you, Lily," Mark said, brushing her long hair away from her face.

"I am too lucky, he is watching me," Lily replied in an excited voice.

"I wanna hear my wife screams," Ethen commented.

"Ahhh, she is amazing by the way," Mark replied pressing her ass.

"Yes honey, fuck me," Lily said excitedly.

Mark could feel the lust in Lily's eyes. She was kissing him madly.

"Take it off," Mark pointed to her black shirt.

"Oh yes," she replied.

There was still a fragrance of flowers in the room. Ethan stepped forward and approached them. He wanted to help them.

Lily took off her shirt and gave it to her husband.

Ethan sniffed her shirt and sat back down in the chair.

The next moment Lily's black bra was in front of him.

"So nice," Mark kissed between her boobs."

"Oh yes..." Lily whispered. Her face turned pale.

Although Lily was wearing a black bra, her boobs were clearly visible.

"I would love to suck your boobs," Mark said and started squeezing her boobs in his hands. Lily closed her eyes.

"Ahhh, Mark, I am getting hot," she murmured.

Ethan's attention was on Lily's face. He was psychologically connected to them. He couldn't take his attention away from Lily and Mark for even a second.

"I love your cooking but now your sexy body is driving me crazy," Mark laughed.

"I am interested in you Mark. I try to prepare the best dishes for you," she was holding his head in her hand.

Ethan smiled. He was enjoying Lily and Mark's closeness.

"You lie down on the bed," Mark ordered her.

Lily looked at Ethan. He winked. Now Lily lay down on the bed. In front of Mark, Ethan's wife was lying on the bed with her hair disheveled. He couldn't quite believe the scene, but what was even more unbelievable to him was that he was going to fuck his wife in front of him.

"I'm going to take your bra off," Mark said softly.

"Mark, that was my greatest wish," Lily smiled.

"You look beautiful when you smile," Mark laughed.

She smiled in response.

"Ahhh, beauty, natural beauty I say," Mark bent down to kiss her.

Meanwhile, Ethan picked up his chair and placed it near the bed. He wanted to see this scene up close.

Mark was leaning over Lily. Ethan was about to watch the scene in silence as Mark took off his wife's bra.

Now Mark held out his hands. He held the strap of her bra and delicately undid it.

"Wow," Ethan commented. He was psychologically connected to the game. Lily was smiling at Ethan.

In the next moment, Mark took off her bra and handed it to Ethan. Ethan was sniffing Lily's bra. The smell of her bra was arousing him. He felt that he should always have such fun with Lily.

In front of Mark were her round, white sexy boobs. Her nipples were dark brown.

"Wow, Amazing" Mark commented. He saw a gold locket on her neck.

This chain was gifted by Ethan to Lily on their first wedding night.

"This is amazing," Mark took her chain in his hand.

"My husband gifted it to me," Lily pointed to Ethan.

Ethan smiled. Lily's bra was still in his hand.

Mark was gently squeezing her boobs. Lily closed her eyes. Ethan could hear her deep breathing. His cock was hard but he felt like he was pressing Lily's boobs instead of Mark.

"Now, I'm gonna lick your boobs," Mark said excitedly. He was sitting on the bed leaning on Lily.

"Oh yeah lick my boobs," Lily opened her eyes.

"Mark Lily is my wife. I love her so much. But tonight is for you," Ethan encouraged him.

"Mark I can't wait to see your cock," Lily looked at Mark.

"It will be a surprise for you," Mark smiled.

"Your smile is my weakness, Mark," Lily held Mark's head and kissed him on the forehead.

Ethan was feeling a little jealous at the sight, but he was also extremely excited that Lily was obsessed with his friend.

Now Mark started sniffing her boobs. The smell of her boobs was driving him crazy. He was kissing Lily's boobs passionately.

"Ah, yes," Lily ran her fingers through his hair.

Ethan was leaning forward watching the scene. His wife's eyes were closed. Lily had abandoned herself to Mark's mercy.

"I wish I could drink milk from your boobs," Mark laughed.

Ethan laughed too.

"Suck my nipples," Lily pulled Mark's head down further.

Now Mark took her dark brown nipples in his mouth and started sucking.

"Oh, my tits..." Lily moaned, but she was holding Mark's head in her hands. Mark began to suck the nipples of the boobs alternately.

Ethan's eyes were sparkling with excitement. He was leaning forward and enjoying.

Even during this, Lily's eyes remained closed, but she continued to moan.

Her moans were a relief to Ethan. Mark was pressing both her boobs while he was expertly sucking the nipples.

"Oh god," Lily screamed excitedly. Their moans in the room excited Ethan. He slipped his hand into his trousers. His cock was hard, but tonight he had given his wife to Mark. He was emotionally attached to this scene.

"Please lick my pussy," Lily looked at Ethan.

"Your boobs are so soft, I love to explore your boobs," Mark said, kissing her nipples.

"Ahhh yes," Lily moaned. Her nipples were hard a little.

"Mark, please make my wife happy. Lick her pussy," Ethan agreed.

Lily smiled and looked at Ethan gratefully.

Now Mark turned towards her jeans. He pulled her jeans a little. Lily had to lift her legs while taking off her jeans. He saw that Lily was also wearing a black thong.

"Oh l have to take it off too," Mark pointed to her thong.

"You have to do everything, my dear," Ethan replied. He was looking at his wife's thong with interest.

"Of course," Lily laughed back.

"Ethan, I am so excited to see your wife's pussy. Ahhh amazing feelings," Mark Addressed to Ethan.

"It is really exciting for me too when you will taste my wife's pussy," Ethan laughed.

"Okay Lily, get ready I am going to take off your jeans," Ethan said kissing her on her belly.

"Yeah, Mark I am so excited," she replied gently.

Lily was still lying down. She put weight on both her feet and raised her ass. At that time Mark pulled her jeans and moved forward. He started sniffing Lily's thong. Lily was holding Marke's head. The smell of her pussy was driving him crazy.

The next moment, he completely took off her jeans. She was wearing only a bra now. Ethan was feeling attraction to his wife as he saw his wife was totally nude in front of his friend.

"Take my thong off with your lips," Lily ordered.

"Good idea," Ethan laughed.

"It is really a tough goal for me," Mark laughed.

"I want to feel every moment," she whispered.

Now Mark grabbed her thong between his lips and pulled but her thong slipped and he could not remove her thong.

"Grab tight," Lily opened her eyes.

Mark now grabbed her thong with his teeth and pulled. Lily's thong was now around her legs which Mark took off completely and threw on Ethan's face. Ethan sniffed his wife's thong. He felt lust rising in him now. Of course, it was all getting better for Lily and Ethan.

"Wow so nice," Mark said as he looked at her beautiful pussy.

A wave of excitement passed through his whole body.

Ethan was also looking at his wife's pussy with lustful eyes. His heart was beating fast.

Because the sexual intensity between him and Lily was over, but when he saw Mark, he decided to have a serious romance with Lily in the future.

Her pussy was pink and shaved. As soon as Mark touched her pussy with his hands, he felt that his cock was fully erect.

"Oh, it's so soft," he whispered.

"Suck my pussy," replied Lily. After Mark's touch, her lust increased.

"Wait honey," Mark replied. He quickly took off his jeans, but Lily kept looking at him with her brown eyes. Soon, Mark had also taken off his underwear.

Ethan and Lily were looking at his big cock.

"Your cock is wonderful," Lily said looking at his cock lustfully.

Ethan was getting a little jealous of Mark's cock, but he was also happy that Mark's cock was going to be a source of sexual satisfaction for his wife.

"Please lick my pussy, Mark," Lily looked at him

"Okay honey," Mark was eager to lick her pussy. He often saw Lily in jeans and a shirt but today he was going to lick her pussy. Ethan was leaning further forward. The candlelight, fragrance of flowers, and semi-darkness made the atmosphere even more impressive.

Mark put both of her legs on his shoulder while his lips were on her wet pussy. He started kissing her pussy gently.

"Oh, yes,,,, Umphhh.." Lily was moaning softly.

Feeling Mark's hot lips on her pussy, her lust was growing. Lily looked at Ethan. Ethan was smiling. It was as if he had joined them as a third partner.

Mark was running his lips over her pussy clits. Her pussy was dripping with salty water, which Mark began to lick with his tongue.

"So tasty," he commented.

Ethan's lust was also increasing. After a long time, he felt the need to lick Lily's pussy. But now his friend Mark was licking his wife's pussy effectively.

"Ah yes, so sweet," Lily cooed excitedly. Her pussy was constantly leaking water which Mark was licking with his tongue.

"I want a whiskey," Lily looked at Ethan.

"Ok I'll bring," Ethan snapped.

He almost ran to the first floor. He took out a bottle of whiskey from the fridge and headed back to the second floor. The night was getting deeper and darker, but it was a magical night for Ethan. As he approached the bedroom. He could hear Lily's excited moans.

"What a beautiful moment. My friend is fucking my wife in my bedroom," Ethan thought and entered the room.

Mark was still licking her pussy. Ethan poured whiskey into a glass and handed it to Lily. The second glass he had filled for Mark.

"Thanks," Mark looked at him with a smile. Mark and Lily clinked their glasses together and in a few seconds, they had emptied their glasses.

"Mark, lick my pussy," Lily said again.

Ethan was back in his chair. Now Mark started licking her pussy again. The sound of pussy licking echoed in the room. Ethan had his eyes on her pussy and Mark's tongue. Mark's cock looked as hard as an iron rod.

"Oh my god, suck please, Mark," Lily breathed deeply.

"So tight," Mark slipped his two fingers into her pussy.

"Ah," Lily laughed hysterically.

Ethan was extremely surprised. Lily had never looked so excited about having sex with him. Ethan's curiosity was growing. He was supporting them in every respect.

Now Mark began to rub the upper part of her pussy with his finger while inserting his tongue in the lower part.

"Oh yes, my pussy" Lily was making random noises. Her eyes were closed but she was feeling Mark's tongue in her pussy.

"Ah, insert your cock in my pussy," Lily almost screamed.

"Oh, yes," Mark spit on her pussy.

Ethan had both hands on the bed. Leaning forward, he watched his wife yearn for Mark's cock.

"Will you lick my cock in front of your husband?" Mark stood up.

Lily opened her eyes. Mark was standing with his cock in his hands. Lily looked at Ethan.

"Yes Lily suck my friend's cock," Ethan ordered her.

Now Lily moved forward. Her long hair was touching her ass.

She took Mark's cock in her hands and spat on it. After making it wet she was massaging it in her hand.

Ethan was enjoying this moment. Her wife was massaging his friend's cock.

"Oh, sweet," Mark moaned.

"I love it," Lily kissed his cock.

"Ah, suck my cock," Mark held her head in his hand.

Lily placed her hot lips on his cock and started kissing.

"Oh, yes, so nice honey," Mark said excitedly.

Ethan was deep in thought. He was thinking that Lily would suck his cock with the same passion in the future.

Lily slowly started licking his cock.

She was sitting on the bed while Mark was standing.

Mark was stroking her hair.

"Suck it, honey," he said, looking up at her face.

Lily was sucking his cock with great pleasure. Sometimes she used to take his cock up to her throat. While doing this, she was making random sounds.

Her mouth was making sexy cock-sucking sounds that Ethan felt like he was going to fuck his wife with the same passion. Ethan's feelings about Lily were changing. Lily was sucking Mark's cock like a thirsty bitch. She was also playing with balls under his cock. Ethan had never seen his wife so excited before. She continued sucking his cock for five minutes. Now Mark's cock was completely wet.

"Turn into doggy style," Mark asked her.

Lily took out Mark's cock from her mouth.

"Will you suck my ass too?" she asked.

"Yeah, honey, I love your soft round ass," Mark replied slapping her ass.

Lily turned into doggy style in front of him.

Ethen was looking at his wife's ass while his friend was ready to suck it.

"I love it," Mark said, slapping Lily's soft ass lovingly.

Her face was on the opposite side. Ethan was looking at her ass. Her long hair was disheveled. Lily looked back at Ethan. Ethan could feel the lust in her eyes.

"Lick my ass," Lily addressed Mark.

Mark started to lick her butt. He was feeling her soft ass with his tongue. While doing so Mark was rubbing her pussy.

"Oh yes, suck my asshole too," she was screaming.

Mark grabbed her butt and put his tongue on her asshole.

"Wow," Ethan said helplessly. He was completely connected in this scene.

Mark started licking her asshole. He was feeling the sharpness of her ass with his hand.

"Ahhh, suck, suck, umphhh," Lily said with difficulty as she was breathing fast.

She was slowly moving her ass back and forth. Ethen was surprised as she was so active while having sex with Mark.

Mark started licking her ass with great pleasure.

"Suck my pussy too," Lily bent down more, and now her head was touching the bedsheet.

Ethen and Mark were looking at her pussy and asshole.

Mark slowly moved down and began to suck her soft and delicate pussy. At that time Lily's passion was at its peak.

"He sucks pretty good," Lily said to Ethan in defiance.

Ethan was seeing a new look of her wife. Lily was absolutely crazy about sex. Ethan had both hands on the bed. He was leaning forward looking closely at his wife's pussy which Mark was licking.

"I'm gonna put my cock in your tight pussy," Mark said, slapping her ass.

He was not able to be patient anymore. He placed his cock on her tight pussy.

These moments were full of excitement for Ethan. He was feeling mixed emotions of love, jealousy, and happiness. He was watching his friend's cock on his wife's pussy. Meanwhile, Lily's eyes were on Ethan. She looked back at

Ethan. Mark was also excited to feel her wet pussy with his cock. He was rubbing his cock on her pussy clits. Ethan was looking at his wife's wet pussy clits. He was feeling attracted to Lily, but her friend's cock was still on his wife's pussy.

"Oh yes, fuck my pussy please," Lily screamed. Feeling Mark's cock on her wet pussy, she became very obsessed.

"So hot," Mark smiled.

He started rubbing his cock on her tight pussy. Her pussy was very wet due to which Mark's cock was sliding easily.

"Insert it in my pussy" Lily said almost screaming.

"Oh, you are so eager," Mark said with a laugh.

Ethan noted that Lily was eager to get Mark's cock in her pussy. Lily's sexual desires were at their peak.

Then he placed his cock on her pussy and gave it a slight jerk. Her pussy was very tight, but half of his cock was in her pussy.

"Oh my god," Lily screamed.

She was more excited to feel his cock in her pussy. She slowly started moving her ass back and forth.

Ethan was watching as his wife was moving her ass to get Mark's big cock in her pussy. She was extremely excited to feel Mark's cock in her pussy. Her hair was bouncing. Mark was breathing deeply now. He was feeling the tightness of her pussy with his cock.

"Your pussy is very tight, ahhh," Mark said while placing his hands on her ass.

However, Lily was silent. She was slowly moving her ass back and forth. While doing so her boobs were bouncing. Meanwhile, Mark took her boobs in his hands and started pressing them.

"Wow my friend has such a sexy lady," Mark whispered.

"Fuck me hard," Lily was screaming.

Mark was sniffing her hair. Ethan was watching his wife's sexy body. His cock was now fully erect.

"Enter the whole cock in my pussy," Lily yelled.

"Ah, it is so wet and tight," Mark slapped her ass and gave a strong shock. His whole cock was entered in her tight pussy.

"Oh, my god" Lily screamed.

Now Mark was rapidly pushing his cock in and out of her pussy. When he also hit her ass, her ass vibrated. Seeing this scene, Ethan was unable to control himself. He moved close and started watching this scene.

"Oh yes. Very nice," Lily sometimes whispered and sometimes her voice rose.

Ethen always fucked her formally, but today he could feel Lily was getting mad. Her boobs were bouncing. Her hair was scattered. The gold chain Ethan had given him was also bouncing.

"Oh Mark, my pussy is yours. Fuck me," Lily cooed.

"Come on Mark," Ethan addressed him.

Now they were enjoying Ethan's presence. Ethan supported them at every opportunity.

Suddenly Mark took out his cock from her pussy.

"What happened? fuck me please" Lily turned back and looked at him.

"Lay down honey," Mark ordered her. Lily lay straight on the bed. Mark put her legs on his cock.

"Give your cock in my hands," Lily asked biting her lower lip. There was excitement in her eyes.

Meanwhile, Lily held his strong cock in her soft hands and put it inside by rubbing it on her pussy.

"Fuck me hard now," she asked excitedly.

Now Mark quickly started to take his cock in and out.

Now Ethan wanted to see the scene more closely. He got up from the chair and sat next to Lily on the bed. He was watching Mark's cock move in and out of his wife's pussy with full attention and interest. Mark was moaning excitedly. He started pumping his cock in and out faster.

"Oh, your pussy is so tight. Awww," Mark almost screamed.

Meanwhile, Lily held Ethan's hand. Ethan looked at Lily in surprise. She was breathing deeply. Ethan could feel his hands trembling. It was the first time Ethan had seen his wife in such a passionate state.

"So sexy lady," Mark grabbed her boobs and started pressing. His balls under his cock were hitting Lily's soft ass.

Lily was on the edge of pleasure by feeling Mark's big cock in her tight pussy.

"Ahhh, god," Lily was moaning due to excitement. Unconsciously, she held Ethan's hand tightly. Ethan was looking more closely at her pussy with lustful eyes. Mark was feeling the depths of her pussy with his cock.

Suddenly he gave a strong jerk. His entire cock was in Lily's tight pussy. He leaned forward and kissed Lily on the face.

"Your pussy is amazing, Lily," he whispered.

"Ah, fuck me," Lily replied. She was moaning.

With Mark's cock still in her pussy he began to suck her boobs and slowly take his cock in and out. Ethan came closer to her pussy. His friend had completely dominated his wife. Mark began to jerk faster. Lily was shivering.

"Oh god, so wet," Mark roared.

At that time, his lust was at its peak. He could hear the sound of her irregular breathing due to which he also moaned excitedly. In the next two minutes, Mark expected that he would ejaculate.

"I am about to cum" Mark said almost roaring.

"Oh, cum on my boobs," Lily replied with a scream.

Meanwhile, Mark moved quickly. He placed his ass on Lily's chest and placed his cock between her boobs and started massaging both the boobs.

"Great, Ethan never tried this," Lily exclaimed excitedly.

"Oh yes, so soft boobs," Mark moaned excitedly.

He was grabbing her boobs tightly and massaging his cock.

"Ah, ah," Lily breathed deeply.

This moment was unforgettable for Ethan as Mark quickly slid his cock between his wife's boobs.

"Ahh, sexy, I am going to cum," Mark roared.

Ethan was very happy that Mark was going to cum on his wife's boobs. He didn't enter his cock between her boobs before. At that moment Ethan thought that he would also do the same thing in the future.

At the same time, a stream of cum came out of Mark's cock, which he discharged on her boobs.

"Oh wow, so warm," Lily saw the cum coming out of Mark's cock.

Ethan noticed Lily's boobs were wet with Mark's cum.

"Wow!" Ethan commented.

"Lick my cum," Mark ordered Lily.

Lily started licking the cum on her boobs with her fingers. Ethan was smiling as he watched Lily licking his friend's cum. Lily's sexual performance was at its peak. Soon she had licked all the cum.

"You are a very good boy, Mark, I really enjoyed it with you," Lily said kissing Mark on the forehead.

"Me too dear" Mark also kissed Lily on the cheek in response. They both hugged each other for a few minutes and lay down.

"Thank you, Mark," Ethan looked at Mark gratefully.

"No need for thanks my dear friend, I really enjoyed with your sexy wife," Ethan replied slapping Lily's ass. Ethan laughed.

Both of them were lying naked on the bed. Lily had one of her legs on the mark. Ethan could still see Lily's wet pussy.

"I'd like a drink dear," Lily ordered Ethan. Her head was on Mark's shoulder. Ethan was a little jealous of the scene, but he had a lot of fun. He once again went to the first floor to bring whiskey. It was past midnight now. Ethan took out a bottle of whiskey from the fridge. Meanwhile, all the scenes that happened a while ago were playing in his mind like an interesting movie. He never thought in his life that he would leave Lily and Mark alone at home, but now it was midnight. Lily and Mark were lying naked in his bedroom on the second floor in his presence and he had gone to get them some whiskey. Although it all seemed strange to Ethan, he was very happy that Lily had been with him since the wedding. He had never looked as eager for sex as she was for Mark tonight. Ethan reached on second floor again.

"Wow my wife is lying naked with my friend and I'm serving him," he mumbled.

He felt very happy, but there was a certain element of Jealousy.

When he reached the door of the room, Mark and Lily were still talking in whispers. Lily lay next to him with her leg still on Mark. Her face was on Mark's chest. Ethan poured whiskey into glasses and handed them. Lily looked dazed.

"Thank you, dear, for a great dinner and your beautiful wife," Mark shook Ethan's hand.

"I enjoyed the scene, too," Ethan replied. They had glasses of whiskey in their hands. Lily was sitting next to Mark. Mark and Lily were completely naked. Mark's legs were touching Lily's ass while Ethan was sitting in front of them.

"Take it, honey," Lily touched her glass to Mark's lips.

Mark smiled and took a sip from Lily's glass. Meanwhile, Ethan was feeling their emotions. For the first time in his life, Ethan had seen his wife with such passion. After emptying Lily's glass, Mark gave her glass to Lily. They were drinking whiskey by each other's hand. Ethan was also drinking whiskey.

Ethan noticed that the candles were starting to go out. After emptying his glass, he lit more candles. Now once again Mark and Lily were lying on the bed. Ethan also laid down on the bed next to Lily. Lily and Mark's dresses were still on the table. Lily lay between Ethan and Mark. She had one leg on Ethan and the other on Mark.

"Lily you were pretty excited today," Ethan whispered.

"Oh yeah, Mark drove me crazy," Lily laughed.

"Lily, I explored every part of your body. You're so beautiful and sexy," Mark said as he placed a few roses on Lily's boobs.

It was a memorable night for Lily, the smell of roses, the light of the candles, and lying between Mark and Ethan. She was thinking about the moments when she waited for Mark. When she sat alone at home, she wrote her thoughts in her diary for Mark. But today Ethan had given her every opportunity to spend the night with Mark.

"Ethan look my pussy is still wet," Lily said holding Ethan on her pussy.

Ethan touched her soft pussy with his hands. Lily's pussy was still wet.

"I felt like we should make our nights memorable as well," Ethan said softly.

"If you'd fuck me the same as Mark, I'd have supported you just as same," Lily replied.

"Your wife is a very sexy lady, Ethan. I've never seen a sexier woman than her," Mark gushed.

"Mark I am proud of my wife. Today I realized she is amazing," Ethan replied.

"Ethan I want you to fuck me like this every night," Lily said lovingly.

"Lily you probably have no idea of my feelings. When Mark was fucking you I wanted to fuck you so hard," Ethan expressed his feelings.

"Thanks, honey, for making my dream come true," Lily hugged him.

Ethan held Lily. Her sexy body was adding to his lust. Lily's breathing started to restore. Ethan was feeling her boobs on his chest.

"Promise Ethan. We'll make our nights colorful like this," Lily whispered.

"I promise. I will always make my wife happy like this," Ethan kissed Lily on the forehead.

"It's a memorable night for me too, Ethan. Tasting your wife's hot pussy after a great dinner," Mark said, hugging Lily from behind.

Lily put her leg on Ethan's leg. Ethan's cock was getting hard. He was fondling her ass. Suddenly his hand collided with Mark's cock. Mark's cock was still touching Lily's pussy.

"Oh your cock is still touching my wife's pussy," Ethan laughed.

"To be honest, I love her soft pussy," Mark also laughed.

Ethan was rubbing Lily's pussy clits with his fingers while Mark moved forward, his cock hitting her pussy.

Ethan pulled Lily closer into a hug.

"Oh, honey I'll be waiting when you fuck me like that," Lily laughed.

"Sure, my love," Ethan kissed her on the forehead.

They were lying and hugging each other. Ethan had been feeling attracted to his wife since tonight. Lily could feel Mark on her back as she hugged Ethan tightly. Ethan was feeling her warm breathing. Lily closed her eyes. Tonight was a memorable night for her. She had a triumphant smile on her face.

The End

Dear reader,

Thank you for reading to the end!

If you want more of these hotwife/cuckold short stories, check out my popular series *Hooked by the BBC*.

Best wishes

Amber

www.ingramcontent.com/pod-product-compliance
Lightning Source LLC
LaVergne TN
LVHW041632070526
838199LV00052B/3323